Noah Saves the Animals

You probably know someone with an animal living at his or her house, don't you? Maybe your friend has a kitty or a puppy. Or perhaps a turtle in a box or a goldfish in a bowl. You might even know someone who has all of these animals living at his or her house.

Can you guess who had the most animals ever to live at his house? If you said anyone living today, you would be wrong.

It was a man who lived a long time ago. In fact, he lived in a huge boat called an ark. He lived there for a year with two of every kind of animal in the world. Can you imagine? You probably know his name by now. That's right. It was Noah.

Little Moorings
Nashville/New York

The Beginners Bible™ and characters licensed exclusively by
Performance Unlimited, Inc., Brentwood, TN.
Produced by Don Wise.
The Beginners Bible™and characters copyright © 1995 by James R. Leininger.
All rights reserved under International and Pan-American Copyright Conventions.
Published in the United States by Little Moorings,
a division of the Ballantine Publishing Group, Random House, Inc., New York,
and simultaneously in Canada by Random House of Canada Limited, Toronto.
Library of Congress Catalog Card Number: 95-79700
ISBN 0-679-87517-4

Manufactured in the United States of America   10 9 8 7 6 5 4 3

LITTLE MOORINGS™ is a trademark of Random House, Inc.

Many years ago there was a time when people began to do lots of bad things. They wouldn't stop. Things were so bad in the world that God decided to start over. And that's exactly what he did.

He looked far and wide for one good man who would help him. Then one day he found Noah and his family. Noah was a very good man who loved God. He worked very hard and he enjoyed life with his family.

God asked Noah to build an ark. Since this was the first boat of its kind in all the world, God explained to Noah what an ark was, and he told him exactly how to build it.

God asked Noah to build the ark three stories high. He told Noah to place a roof on the ark and a wide door in the side.

Noah built the ark of gopher wood. He put lots of rooms in it and painted it with pitch so that no water would seep inside.

Then God said to Noah, "You and your family will live on the ark, where I will keep you safe until the flood is over."

Now, Noah had a wife. He also had three sons, and they had wives. They would all live together on the ark.

God wanted to save Noah and his family, and God wanted to save the animals, too.

Noah was being asked to do a very big job! How would he do it? How would he gather so many animals into the ark? How would he feed all of them? How could he love them all? And who would help him?

Noah wanted to save the animals. He knew his wife would help. He knew his sons and their wives would help. But most of all, Noah knew God would help.

Then a great thing happened. All the animals started coming to the ark, two by two. What a sight to see! And what a sound to hear!

The earth rumbled and the heavens rang as all the animals started coming.

Racing as fast as they could, the rabbits leaped right over the poky turtles. Next were the long-necked giraffes, just in front of the ostriches. The striped zebras darted past, with the horses not far behind.

Noah watched as all the large animals began to arrive.
There were big, burly bears, roaring lions, and fierce tigers
all standing side by side.

There were so many different kinds of animals that Noah could hardly believe his eyes. The heavy hippos lumbered along right beside the gliding, graceful gazelles. The broad-tailed kangaroos hopped by while the field mice scampered up the trail.

The ducks waddled in, and the proud peacocks strutted behind. The monkeys were riding on the elephants.

Can you imagine such a sight? And what sounds! The tiny puppy dogs were yapping and the cats were meowing. The cows were mooing and the rooster was crowing. "Here we come," they all seemed to say. "There's room for all of you," Noah said with a smile.

Then God said to Noah, "In seven days, I will send rain." It was time for Noah to load his family, food, and all of the animals onto the ark.

Noah did everything God told him to do. All of the animals and all of Noah's family were safe inside the ark. Then God shut the door and it began to rain.

It rained and rained and rained some more. The water lifted the ark higher and higher above the earth. It rained for forty days and forty nights.

Finally, the rain stopped. The ark floated for a long, long time. Noah sent a dove to search for dry land. The dove returned because it could not find a dry place to rest. Water still flooded the land.

Time passed, and Noah sent the dove out a second time. The dove returned with an olive branch. Noah knew the water was going down. Soon he would see land.

Once again, Noah sent out the dove. When the dove did not return, Noah knew it was time to leave the ark.

The ark came to rest on a mountaintop. Noah and his family came out of the ark. Then all the animals came out.

Noah thanked God for keeping his family and all the animals safe.
God put a rainbow in the sky. The rainbow was God's promise to never
flood the earth again.